Selected from

KRAMER
VS.
KRAMER

Avery Corman

Supplementary material by the staff of
Literacy Volunteers of New York City

Writers' Voices
Literacy Volunteers of New York City

Selected from

KRAMER

VS.

KRAMER

Avery Corman

WRITERS' VOICES™ was made possible by grants from
The Booth Ferris Foundation, The Vincent Astor Foundation,
and The Scripps-Howard Foundation.

.   .   .

ATTENTION READERS: We would like to hear what you
think about our books. Please send your comments or
suggestions to:

The Editors
Literacy Volunteers of New York City
666 Broadway, #520
New York, NY 10012

.   .   .

Selection: From KRAMER VS. KRAMER by Avery Corman.
Copyright © 1977 by Avery Corman. Reprinted by permission
of the author and Random House, Inc., 201 East 50 Street,
New York, NY 10022.

Supplementary materials © 1989 by Literacy Volunteers of
New York City Inc.

Photo credits: Courtesy of *The New York Times*

Printed in The United States of America

96 95 94 93 92 91 90   10 9 8 7 6 5 4 3 2 1

First LVNYC Printing: January 1989

ISBN 0-929631-01-3

Writers' Voices is a series of books published by Literacy
Volunteers of New York City Inc., 666 Broadway, New
York, NY 10012. The words, "Writers' Voices," are a
trademark of Literacy Volunteers of New York City.
Designed by Paul Davis Studio

Acknowledgments

Literacy Volunteers of New York City gratefully
acknowledges the generous support of the following
foundations which made the publication of WRITERS'
VOICES and NEW WRITERS' VOICES possible:
The Booth Ferris Foundation, The Vincent Astor
Foundation, and The Scripps-Howard Foundation.
We also wish to thank Hildy Simmons, Linda L.
Gillies, and David Hendin for their assistance.

This book could not have been realized without the
kind and generous cooperation of the author, Avery
Corman, and his publisher, Random House, Inc. We
are particularly grateful to Mr. Corman for writing a
special note to the reader for this book.

We deeply appreciate the contributions of the following
suppliers: Cam Steel Rule Die Works, Inc. (steel
cutting die for display); Domtar Industries Inc. (text
stock); Federal Paper Board Company, Inc. and
Milton Paper Company Inc. (cover stock); Jackson
Typesetting (text typesetting); Lancer Graphic
Industries Inc. (cover printing); Martin/Friess
Communications (display header); Mergenthaler Container
(corrugated display); Offset Paperback Mfrs., Inc., A
Bertelsmann Company (text printing and binding); and
Stevenson Photo Color Company (cover color
separations).

For their guidance and assistance, we wish to thank
the *Writers' Voices* Advisory Committee: committee
chair James E. Galton, Marvel Comics; Jeff Brown;
George P. Davidson, Ballantine Books; Susan
Kaminsky; Parker B. Ladd, Association of American
Publishers; Jerry Sirchia, Association of American

Publishers; Benita Somerfield; and Irene Yuss, New American Library.

In the planning stages of this series, the following volunteer tutors and staff members were most helpful in testing the concepts: Betty Ballard, Louisa Brooke, Dan Cohen, Marilyn Collins, Ann Keniston, Elizabeth Mann, Gary Murphy, Isabel Steinberg, and June Wilkins.

For generously giving of their time and expertise, we want to thank F. Robert Stein (legal advice); Gene Durante (operations advice); Jacque Cook, Sharon Darling, Donald Graves, Doris Gunderson, Renée Lerche, and Dorothy Strickland (peer reviewers); and Pat Fogarty, Kathleen Gray, and Ingrid Strauch (copyediting and proofreading).

Our thanks to Paul Davis Studio and Claudia Bruno, José Conde, Myrna Davis, Paul Davis, and Jeanine Esposito for the inspired design of the books and their covers. We would also like to thank Barbara A. Mancuso of *The New York Times* Pictures for her help with photo research and selection.

For their marketing assistance and support, our thanks to the Mass Market Education Committee of the Association of American Publishers. For her publicity skills, we thank Barbara J. Hendra of Barbara Hendra Associates.

LVNYC staff members Gary Murphy and Sarah Wilkinson made numerous helpful suggestions. And finally, special credit must be given to Marilyn Boutwell and Jean Fargo of the LVNYC staff for their major contributions to the educational and editorial content of these books.

Contents

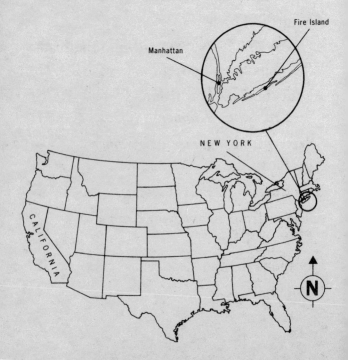

Fire Island

Manhattan

NEW YORK

CALIFORNIA

N

About *Writers' Voices*

"I want to read what others do—what I see people reading in libraries, on the subway, and at home."

Mamie Moore, a literacy student,
Brooklyn, New York

Writers' Voices is our response to Mamie Moore's wish:

the wish to step forward into the reading community,
the wish to have access to new information,
the wish to read to her grandchildren,
the wish to read for the joy of reading.

Note to the Reader

"What we are familiar with, we cease to see. The writer shakes up the familiar scene, and as if by magic, we see a new meaning in it."

Anaïs Nin

Writers' Voices invites you to discover new meaning. One way to discover new meaning is to learn something new. Another is to see in a new way something you already know. Writers touch us by writing about familiar things—love, family, death, for example. Even if the experiences in a book are different from our own, the emotions may be familiar. Our own thoughts and feelings let us interact with the author's story.

Writers' Voices is a series of books. Each book contains unedited selections from one writer's work. We chose the selections because the writers' voices can be clearly heard. Also, they deal with experiences that are interesting to think about and discuss.

If you are a new reader, you may want to have a selection read aloud to you, perhaps more than once. This will free you to enjoy the piece, to hear the language used, and to think about its meaning. Even if you are a more experienced reader, you may enjoy hearing the selection read aloud before reading it silently to yourself.

Each selection is set in a framework to expand your understanding of the selection. The framework includes a chapter that tells about the writer's life. Some authors write about their own lives; other authors write stories from their imagination. You may wonder why an author chose to write what he or she did. Sometimes you can find the answer by knowing about the author's life.

You may also find chapters about the characters, the plot, and when or where the story took place. These will help you begin thinking about the selection. They will also help you understand what may be unfamiliar to you.

We believe that to be a reader, you must be at the center of the reading process. We believe you learn best when you choose what you will read. We encourage you to read *actively*. An active reader does many things—while reading, and before and after reading—that help him or her better understand and enjoy a book. Here are some suggestions of things you can do:

Before Reading

- Read the front and back covers of the book, and look at the cover illustration. Think about what you expect the book to be about, based on this information.
- Think about why you want to read this book.
- Ask yourself what you want to discover, and what questions you hope will be answered.
- Think about how your own experiences and knowledge can help you better understand the book.

During Reading
- Try to stay with the rhythm of the language. If you find any words or sentences you don't understand, keep reading to see if the meaning becomes clear. If it doesn't, go back and reread the difficult part or discuss it with others. If you prefer to wait until you have read the whole story before you reread the difficult part, underline it so it will be easy to find later.
- Put yourself into the story. If you feel left out, ask why. Is it the writing? Is it something else?
- Ask yourself questions as you read. For example: Do I believe this story or this character? Why?

After Reading
- Ask yourself if the story makes you see any of your own experiences in a new way.
- Ask yourself if the story has given you any new information.
- Keep a journal in which you can

write down your thoughts about what you have read, and save new words you have learned.

- Discuss what you have read with others.

Good writing should make you think after you put the book down. Whether you are a beginning reader, a more experienced reader, or a teacher of reading, we encourage you to take time to think about these books and to discuss your thoughts with others.

When you finish a selection, you may want to choose among the questions and suggested activities that follow. They are meant to help you discover more about what you have read and how it relates to you—as a person, as a reader, and as a writer.

When you are finished with the book, we hope you will write to our editors about your reactions. We want to know your thoughts about our books, and what they have meant to you.

About Avery Corman

Avery Corman was born on November 28, 1935, in New York City. He has written many plays and books. In 1971, his first novel, *Oh, God!*, became a bestseller. It was later made into a movie starring George Burns and John Denver. Avery Corman also wrote *Kramer vs. Kramer*, another novel that became a bestseller and a movie.

Avery Corman lives in New York City with his wife, Judy. They have two sons, Matthew and Nicholas. Mr. Corman has been an active supporter of the literacy cause. He has organized readings and fund-raising events to aid literacy programs. For this book, he has written a special introduction for people who are learning about writing.

Special Note to the Reader
from Avery Corman

When I start to write a novel, it is not because I have "a good idea." My books never begin with ideas, they begin with feelings. If I feel so strongly about something that I have to write it down, then I have the starting point for a novel.

This was the case with *Kramer vs. Kramer*. I had become a father and I wanted to express what fatherhood meant to me—the deep feelings of love for a child, of fear that I might not be a good father, of concern about being able to provide for my family, of pride that a man could be as loving a parent as a woman. All these feelings went into the writing of *Kramer vs. Kramer*.

It takes me a long time to write a novel, sometimes a couple of years. During this time, I work at a regular pace, a work day like other workers, starting after breakfast, taking a break for lunch, stopping before dinner. I don't usually work nights or weekends, but I do put in a full five-day work week.

My writing goes through many changes. I write and rewrite and rewrite some more. After I type it out, I scribble between the lines, in the margins, all over the page. My handwriting is terrible. I always worry that when I go back to look at something I did months before, I won't be able to read my own writing. This happens, but not often. Since I am able to figure out my writing when nobody else can, I usually retype my work myself.

The point of this is: Writing isn't an easy process. Everything I write goes through many stages. Sometimes there is a thought, an idea that I just can't seem to express the way I want. It escapes my grasp and I never get it right. Sometimes there is a beautiful phrase or sentence or idea that I just cannot express because of my own limitations. But I just try to keep going, doing the best that I can with the voice that I have.

About the Movie
Kramer vs. Kramer

Avery Corman's novel *Kramer vs. Kramer* was made into a movie starring Dustin Hoffman and Meryl Streep. *Kramer vs. Kramer* won the 1979 Academy Award for Best Picture, and Dustin Hoffman won that year's Best Actor award.

Many movies are based on stories that first appeared in books. Movie producers read many books in their search for a good story. When they find a story they like, they must buy from the author the right to make it into a movie. Sometimes the author writes the script.

If you want to know if a movie is based on a book, read the credits at the beginning or end of the film. The title of the book and the author's name will be listed. *Gone with the Wind, The Godfather,* and *The Color Purple* are a few of the many famous movies that started out as books.

Who Gets the Children?

This chapter provides a background for the selection.

Divorce, or separation from a lover, is a very upsetting experience. The experience is even harder when there are children.

First, the parents must decide who the child, or children, will live with. Many people think that it should always be the mother. But sometimes the father is the better person.

In almost 90% of homes where there is only one parent, that parent is the mother. But people who have studied parenting believe that a father can be as good as a mother at raising children. These people believe that the way to decide which parent should raise a child is to see which parent wants to do it the most.

Many divorced parents share the care of the children, perhaps with each taking the children half of the time. Others split up the children, each child staying with the parent who can help him or her the most.

Because of some people's beliefs, a mother might be made to feel guilty if she didn't choose to care for her children. Her friends and her family might make her think she was not a good person. But some mothers do not want to have the children, at least not all the time.

One reason a mother might feel this way is that she doesn't think she has enough money to care for the children. Another reason might be that she needs to spend more time on her job or education. A third reason might be that she feels a need to be on her own for a while. Yet another reason might be that the children get along better with their father.

When parents are divorcing, the custody of the children is decided by the parents and a judge. This is part of the legal process of divorce. Each state has different laws dealing with custody. Judges consider the children's wishes, as well as the best interests of the children. In recent years, the trend has been to give the parents joint custody, allowing each of them to share in raising the children.

Kramer vs. Kramer changed the way many people look at divorce and parenthood. The story made people realize that a father's custody can be good for a child. It showed that a father's care can be as loving and nurturing as a mother's.

About the Selection from
Kramer vs. Kramer

Kramer vs. Kramer is the story of Joanna and Ted Kramer and their son Billy, who is four years old. They live in New York City.

Joanna believes her marriage is suffocating her. She thinks she no longer has anything in common with Ted. She wants to get a job instead of staying home with Billy. She feels she is not a good mother.

Joanna is very unhappy with her life and can't take it anymore. She tells Ted that she is leaving him, and Billy as well. She thinks Billy will be better off with Ted.

Ted must deal with his surprise at Joanna's feelings and his sadness over the end of his marriage. He must also help Billy understand what has happened. And he must learn to be both mother and father to Billy.

Perhaps the story will make you think

about whether fathers make as good single parents as mothers. Or perhaps it will make you think about what a child might feel about divorce or being abandoned.

A street in New York City similar to the street where Ted and Billy live (Credit: Marilyn K. Yee/ *The New York Times*)

Selected from

Kramer vs. Kramer

Part One

He fell asleep near five in the morning realizing there would be no key in the door or phone call with an apology— I'll be right there, I love you. At seven-fifteen he heard voices in the house. Joanna? No. Batman and Robin. Billy's Batman and Robin alarm clock went off with the recorded voices of the dynamic duo: "Jumping Jehosophat, Batman, we're needed again." "Right, Robin. We have to wake our friends." For what? To begin where? She had left this with him and now he had to tell Billy. Tell him what?

"Where's Mommy?" He could not avoid it even thirty seconds into the day.

"Well, last night Mommy and Daddy had an argument ..." Was this even true, he wondered. Had they argued? "And Mommy decided she wants to go

away for a little while to be really angry.
You know, how sometimes you get angry and you slam your door and you
don't want anybody to come in?"

"I was angry when Mommy wouldn't
let me have a cookie."

"Right."

"And I slammed the door and I didn't
let her come in."

"Right, just like that. Mommy is angry at Daddy and she wants some time
to be private."

"Oh."

"So I'm going to take you to school
today."

"Oh. When will Mommy be back?"

"I'm not sure."

"Will she pick me up at school?"

They were now but a minute into the
day and it was already complicated. . . .

At night, Ted and Billy followed the
adventures of Babar the Elephant to New
York, to Washington, to another planet.
Was Joanna in any of these places? And

weary from Babar's travels, Ted turned out the light. A half-hour later, when Ted thought Billy had already gone to sleep, he called out from his room.

"Daddy, when is my mommy coming back?"

Why were children always so damn direct, he wondered.

"I don't know, Billy. We'll figure something out."

"What, Daddy?"

"We'll see. Go to sleep. Tomorrow is Saturday. We'll go on the bike to the zoo and have fun. Think about that—"

"Can I have pizza?"

"You can have pizza."

"Good."

The boy fell asleep content. They went to the zoo and Billy had an outstanding day, conning the pizza out of his father by eleven in the morning. He got a pony cart ride, a carrousel ride, they went to a local playground, he climbed, made a friend. Then Ted took Billy out for Chinese food for dinner. Ted was treading water. He was going to have to deal with this, make some decisions. He could play this out for only another day perhaps and then it was Monday, he had a job to be at—unless he took some vacation days to gain more time. Joanna could come back, call.

At eight in the morning on Sunday, the mailman came with a special delivery letter. It was for Billy with no return address. The postmark was Denver, Colorado.

"This is from your mommy to you."

"Read it to me, Daddy."

The letter was written by hand. Ted read it slowly so that Billy could absorb it, and so that he could.

> My dear, sweet Billy: Mommy has gone away. Sometimes in the world, daddys go away and the mommys bring up their little boys. But sometimes a mommy can go away, too, and you have your daddy to bring you up. I have gone away because I

must find some interesting things to do for myself in the world. Everybody has to and so do I. Being your mommy was one thing and there are other things and this is what I have to do. I did not get a chance to tell you this and that is why I am writing to you now, so you can know this from me. Of course, I will always be your mommy and I will send you toys and birthday cards. I just won't be your mommy in the house. But I will be your mommy of the heart. And I will blow you kisses that will come to you when you are sleeping. Now I must go and be the person I have to be. Listen to your daddy. He will be like your wise Teddy. Love, Mommy.

Ted allowed for an instant the pain it must have caused her to write it, measured by the pain it caused him to read it. Billy took the letter to hold in his hands. Then he put it in his drawer where he kept his special coins and birthday cards.

"Mommy went away?"

"Yes, Billy."

"Forever, Daddy?"

Goddamn you, fucking Joanna! Goddamn you!

"It looks that way, Billy."

"She's going to send me toys?"

"Yes, she's going to send you toys."

"I like toys."

It was official. She was gone to both of them. . . .

The next day, a brief note came to Ted, again without a forwarding address, this time with a Lake Tahoe, Nevada, postmark.

"Dear Ted: There is a certain amount of legal shit. I'm having a lawyer send papers regarding our pending divorce. Also am sending you documents you need for legal custody of Billy. Joanna."

He thought it to be the ugliest note he had ever seen in his life.

The beach at Fire Island (Credit: *The New York Times*)

Introduction to Part Two of the Selection from *Kramer vs. Kramer*

After caring for Billy for over a year and a half, Ted has learned a great deal about being a parent. He has been through good and bad times with Billy, and they have grown very close.

When Joanna left them, she moved to California. While she was away, she only visited Billy once. Now she has moved back to New York City so that she can get custody of Billy.

Ted refuses to let Joanna have custody. He doesn't think it is fair that she thinks she can suddenly come back and say she has changed her mind.

Joanna takes Ted to court to settle who should have custody of Billy. Joanna tells the judge that she loves Billy and wants to be with him. She also thinks Billy needs to be with his mother more than he needs to be with his father.

Ted tells the judge how much he

loves Billy and how he wants things to stay as they are. Ted has witnesses who tell the judge what a good father he is. One of the witnesses is Etta, the woman who takes care of Billy when Ted is at work.

When everyone has spoken, the judge must decide who gets custody. Basing his decision on past judgments, the judge decides that a child as young as Billy should live with his mother.

Ted must now deal with his sadness at losing custody of Billy. He must also try to explain to Billy what has happened. Perhaps you will want to think about how the judge's decision will affect Billy, Ted, and Joanna.

Selected from

Kramer vs. Kramer

Part Two

Etta returned from food shopping and Ted informed her that Joanna had been awarded custody of the boy. The time she had spent with Billy had been invaluable, he said, and Billy would always have a good foundation from the love she had given him. He had decided to make a request of Joanna that she retain Etta as a housekeeper, and Etta said of course she would be willing to take care of Billy. Then she got busy in the house, putting away food. A little while later he heard her. She was in the bathroom, crying.

Billy was to be finished with his school day shortly, and Ted asked Etta to take him to the park for a while. He had unfinished business and he could not bear to see him just now. He began making phone calls to tell people, hop-

ing to reach secretaries, third parties,
answering machines, preferring to just
leave messages and not have to get into
conversations. He thought it would be
best to leave the city for the weekend as
planned, for Saturday and Sunday any-
way. Ted could get away from the phone,
and Billy would be deeply disappointed
if the adventure were canceled. After he
left his messages, spoke to friends, shared
their regrets, he called his mother. Dora
Kramer did not howl as he expected she
might. "Joanna won custody," he told her,
and she said quietly, "I was afraid of that."

"Will I never see him again?" she
asked, and Ted was not clear for the
moment how visitation rights worked
for grandparents.

"I promise you, Mother, you'll see him.
If nothing else, on my time."

"My poor baby," she said. He was
about to answer her with some invented
reassurance about Billy, when she said,
"What will you do?" and he realized his
mother was referring to him.

The question of Etta was an immediate concern to Ted. He wanted to get to Joanna before she made plans. If he mailed a special-delivery letter immediately, Joanna would have it in the morning. He did not care to speak to her. There were other things to be communicated about Billy, as well. He could not pin a note to his jacket as though the child were a refugee. He wrote:

Joanna—This is by way of introducing William Kramer. He is a sweet child, as you will see. He is allergic to grape juice, but will more than make up for the loss in apple juice. He is not, however, allergic to grapes. Don't ask me why. He seems to also be allergic to peanut butter from the health food store, fresh ground, but not the stuff they sell in the supermarket—and don't ask me why. At times, in the night he will be visited by monsters, or one particular monster. It is called The

Face. The Face, as best I can determine, looks like a circus clown without a body, and from what the pediatrician says, and what I have read, may be a sexual fear of losing his penis, or a fear of his own anger, or just a circus clown he saw once. His doctor, by the way, is Feinman. His best medicine for colds is Sudafed. His best stories have been Babar and Winnie the Pooh up to now, with Batman moving up. His housekeeper has been Etta Willewska and is a main reason for this note. She is a loving woman, conscientious, very concerned about Billy, experienced, anything you'd want in a housekeeper. Most important, Billy cares for her and is used to her. I hope you don't feel the need to make such a clean slate that you won't consider her. I urge you to retain her. Her number is 555-7306, and I think she will take the job if offered. I'm sure other things will come up. Ask me what you need to and I guess eventually we'll talk. That's all I can think of right now. Try to speak well of me in his presence, and I will try, against my feelings, to do the same for you, since it would be "in the best interests of the child," as they say. Ted.

He mailed it special delivery from the post office and then went home to wait for Billy. The boy came into the house, his face rosy from the outdoors. He rushed to Ted—"Daddy, you're home so early," hugging his father around his waist. He could not tell the boy then that he no longer lived there, nor could he tell him at dinner, a last Burger King, or at bedtime, with Billy turning out all the lights to test his "superpowered raccoon-spotting flashlight." Ted delayed through breakfast the next day, and finally, unable to put it off any longer, while waiting for Larry and

Ellen to call for them, he made the speech.

"Billy, you know your mommy now lives in New York City?"

"I know."

"Well, sometimes when a mother and a father are divorced, there is a discussion about who the child should live with, the mother or the father. Now, there is a man who is very wise. He's called a judge. And the judge has a lot of experience with divorces and mothers and fathers and children. He decides who it would be best for the child to live with."

"Why does he decide?"

"Well, that's what he does. He's a very powerful man."

"Like a principal?"

"Bigger than a principal. The judge sits in robes in a big chair. This judge has thought a lot about us, about you and me and Mommy, and he has decided that it would be best for you if you live with Mommy in her apartment.

And I'm very lucky. Because even though you live with Mommy, I'll get to see you every Sunday."

And I will, Billy, I promise you. . . .

"I don't understand, Daddy."

Neither do I.

"What part of it don't you understand, honey?"

"Where will my bed be, where will I sleep?"

"At Mommy's. She'll have a bed for you in your own room."

"Where will my toys be?"

"We'll send your toys there, and I'm sure you'll get some new ones."

"Who will read me my stories?"

"Mommy."

"Will Mrs. Willewska be there, too?"

"Now, that I don't know about. That's still being discussed."

"Will you come and say good night to me every night?"

"No, Billy. I'll still live here. I'll see you on Sundays."

"I'll live in Mommy's house?"

"And it will all start this Monday. Your mommy will come for you in the morning and pick you up here."

"But we were supposed to go for the weekend! You promised!"

"We'll still go. We'll come home a day earlier, that's all."

"Oh, that's good."

"Yes, that's good."

The child took a few moments to evaluate the information, then he said:

"Daddy, does this mean we'll never play monkeys again?"

Oh, Jesus, I don't think I can get through this.

"Yes, my honey, we'll play monkeys again. We'll just be Sunday monkeys."

On the car ride to Long Island, the grownups worked desperately for a jolly beginning to the weekend, singing "I've Been Working on the Railroad" and other favorites. In the interludes between the forced merriment, Ellen would glance back at Ted and Billy and then turn away, unable to look. Given the slightest break from the songs, everyone above the age of five and a half was solemn. Billy was talking away, fascinated by the off-season life on the island: "Where do the birds go?" "Do children live there?" "Does the ferry crash into the ice like an icebreaker boat?" and then, he, too, would fall silent, thinking.

"Daddy, I have a secret." And he whispered so the others would not hear. "What if The Face comes when I live at Mommy's?"

"Mommy knows about The Face. You and Mommy will tell The Face to beat it."

On the ferry ride across, Billy looked out the window, not wanting to miss even a wave in his adventure, and then his interest would drop, apprehensions would take him over again.

"Does Mommy know I can't drink grape juice?"

"Yes, she knows. She won't give you anything that's not good for you."

When they reached the island, Billy

converted the empty summer houses into "Ghostland," creating a game which he and Ted played through the morning, searching for ghosts, climbing on and off decks of houses, scaring each other, laughing. Don't make this too wonderful, Ted was thinking. Maybe it's better if we go out on a shitty time.

The child's enthusiasm was infectious. After lunch, Larry and Ellen, lightened by the rum the adults had been drinking on this cloudy, cold day, played Ghostland also. Then they all jogged along the beach. After dinner, Billy took his flashlight out to look for small animals, but Ghostland was suddenly legitimate. He lasted outside in the dark for only ten minutes, driven indoors by shadows and night sounds.

"Did you see any deer?" Larry asked. "There are deer on the island, you know."

"Not in Ocean Bay Park," Ted said. "They won't rent to them."

They began to laugh, Billy also, who thought it was very funny.

"Can you imagine if the deer shopped in the grocery?" Billy said, a joke by a five-year-old, and on laughter and rum and the long day outside, they all fell asleep in their sleeping bags, chuckling to the end.

Sunday, the last day, Ted and Billy bundled up and went down to the beach to build a sandcastle. The beach was empty. They were on an island of their own this one last time. They tossed a ball on the beach, took a walk to the bay and sat on the dock, finally going inside to get away from the raw weather. Ted and Billy played pickup sticks, the boy intent on the game, and then as before, his mind began to drift again. He suddenly turned and looked at his father with lost eyes. Ted Kramer knew that he had to be the daddy now, no matter how deep his own pain, he had to help the boy get through this.

"You're going to be fine, Billy. Mommy loves you. And I love you. And you can tell anybody just what it is you want, whatever it is."

"Sure, Dad."

"You'll be just fine. You're surrounded by people who love you."

On the ferry back, no one was laughing any more. For Ted, the pain of their separation was so intense he could hardly breathe.

In the city, Larry and Ellen dropped them off at the house. "Hang in, buddy," Larry said to Ted. Then Ellen kissed Billy and told him, "You're welcome to visit us on the island any time. You remember that. We'll look for deer in the grocery."

"It will have to be on a Sunday," the boy said, grasping the reality completely.

Ted saw that Billy brushed his teeth, got into his pajamas, then he read him a story. He said good night, keeping it cheery. "See you in the morning, Billy." He tried to watch a movie on television, but he was, thankfully, exhausted. And then he took one final look at the boy sleeping. Had he invested too much in the child, he wondered. Perhaps somewhat, he thought. But as he had come to believe, a certain amount of this was inevitable when you were alone with a child. Joanna would find it the same. He decided it was just as it should have been during these many months. He was grateful for this time. It had existed. No one could ever take it away. And he felt he was not the same for it. He believed he had grown because of the child. He had become more loving because of the child, more open because of the child, stronger because of the child, kinder because of the child, and had experienced more of what life had to offer—because of the child. He leaned over and kissed him in his sleep and said, "Goodbye, little boy. Thank you."

They had several hours before Joanna would arrive.

"What do you say we go out for breakfast this morning, kiddo?"

"Do I get a donut?"

"After." Ted Kramer had picked up all the parental shorthand.

They went to a neighborhood luncheonette and sat in a booth—breakfast out. Soon he would be like the other Sunday fathers, looking for things to do—out. They returned to the apartment and packed Billy's most important belongings into two suitcases. There was nothing to do now but wait for Joanna. Ted allowed Billy to watch morning television in Ted's bedroom, while he read the newspaper in the living room.

Joanna was late. It was ten-fifteen. The least she could have done this one day was make it as painless as possible, he thought. By ten-thirty, he was pacing. A really shitty thing to do, Joanna! By eleven, he realized he did not even have her phone number. The number was unlisted. He tried to locate Ron Willis and could not. At eleven-twenty, the phone finally rang.

"Ted?"

"Goddamn it, Joanna!"

"I'm sorry."

"Where the hell are you?"

"Home."

"For Christ's sake!"

"Ted, I'm not coming."

"You're—"

"I can't make it."

"Joanna!"

"I just can't make it."

"What is this, Joanna?"

"I—can't—get it together."

"You can't get it together?"

"I can't."

"You mean this morning, today? What the hell are you saying, goddammit?"

"I can't ... I just can't." And she started to cry.

"What can't you?"

"I mean ... sitting in the courtroom ... hearing what you've done ... what's involved..." He could barely make out her words. "The responsibilities ..."

"What about it? Joanna, what about it?"

"My head just isn't there."

"Joanna, I have a boy here with his bags packed!"

"He's a lovely boy—"

"Yes, he is."

"A lovely boy."

"Joanna—"

"I thought it could be different. But when it comes down to it ... I mean, faced with actually doing it—"

"What? *What*, goddammit?"

"I guess I'm not a very together person. I guess ... the things that made me leave are ... still a part of me. I don't have very good feelings about myself just now."

"Joanna, what are you saying? Where *are* we for Christ's sake?"

"I can't make it, Ted. I can't commit to—"

"Joanna!"

"He's ... yours, Ted."

"He's mine?"

"I did want him. I really did—"

"Do you mean this?"

"I'm not coming, Ted. I'm not show-ing up."

"Is this for true?"

"I won't fight you for him any more."

"I can have Billy?"

"I don't think any judge would object now ..." And she trailed off into deep sobbing.

"Oh, Ted ... Ted ... Ted ... Ted ..."

"Easy, Joanna—"

"You know, I guess I am a failure. I'm a failure, just like your lawyer said."

"Jesus—the things we've done to each other."

"You can have him, Ted. He's yours."

"He's really mine?"

"Yes, Ted."

"Oh, my—"

"Only ... could I ask you something?"

"What, Joanna?"

"Could I see him sometimes?"

She was so vulnerable at this mo-ment, he felt he could annihilate her with a word. By his just saying no, she would go away. But it was not in him to do so, nor did he feel he had the right.

"We'll work something out."

"Thank you, Ted. I . . . just can't talk any more." And she hung up.

He leaned back against the wall, so overcome that his legs could not even support his weight. He sat down at the dining room table, numb, shaking his head, trying to believe it. Billy was his. After all this, he was his. He sat there, tears streaming down his face.

Once Etta had told him he was a very lucky man. He was feeling this now, joy and thankfulness and that he was truly a very lucky man. He got up and walked over to the packed suitcases which were standing in the foyer, and still crying, he carried them back into the boy's room.

Billy was watching television. He needed to be told. Ted tried to compose himself, then he went inside, turned the television set off and kneeled in front of the boy.

"Billy, Mommy just called. And . . .

well, Billy ... you're going to live here
with me, after all."

"Mommy's not coming?"

"Not today. She loves you. She loves
you a lot. But it's going to be the way
it's been."

"It is?"

"Because I love you, too, Billy." His eyes
filled with tears again. "And ... I would
have been ... very lonely without you."

"You mean I'll still sleep in my bed?"

"Yes. In your room."

"And all my toys will stay?"

"Yes."

"And my Batman?"

"Yes."

"And my books?"

"Everything."

The child tried to register it.

"So I'm not going there today?"

"That's right, Billy."

"Are you working today?"

"No."

"Then can we go to the playground,
Daddy?"

"Yes, Billy. We can go to the play-ground."

They did ordinary things that day, went to the playground, brought back a pizza, watched *The Muppets,* Billy went to bed, and Ted Kramer got to keep his son.

Your Thoughts about the Selection from *Kramer vs. Kramer*

1. What did you think of the selection from *Kramer vs. Kramer*? Did you like it? Why?

2. Are there ways that the events or people in the selection became important or special to you? Write or discuss why.

3. What parts of the selection were the most interesting? Why?

4. Was the ending what you expected it would be? If not, what did you expect and why?

5. Was there anything new or surprising to you in the selection? What?

QUESTIONS FOR THE READER

Thinking about the Story

1. Describe the people in the selection from *Kramer vs. Kramer*. Which do you think is the most important? Why?

2. Letters are important in this story. How do these letters help you understand how Ted and Joanna feel about each other and about Billy?

3. In some fiction, *where* the story takes place is important. This story takes place in a city. In what ways is the place important or not important to the story?

4. As you were listening or reading, what were your thoughts as the story unfolded?

5. Were any parts of the selection difficult to understand? If so, you may want to read or listen to them again. You might think about why they were difficult.

Thinking about the Writing

1. How did Avery Corman help you see, hear, and feel what happened in the story? Find the words, phrases, or sentences that you think did this the best.

2. Writers think about their stories' settings, characters, and events. In writing this story, which of these things do you think Avery Corman felt was most important? Find the parts of the story that support your opinion.

3. Which character was most interesting to you? How did Avery Corman help you learn about this person? Find the places in the selection where you learned the most about this person.

4. In the selection, Avery Corman uses dialogue. Dialogue can make a story stronger and more alive. Pick out some dialogue that you feel is strong, and explain how it helps the story.

5. The selection is written from the point of view of someone outside the story who tells us what is happening. The writer uses the words "he" and "she." How would the writing be different if the story was told from a different point of view (such as Billy's)?

6. In this story, Avery Corman makes you feel Ted's and Billy's emotions in many ways. Go back to the story and see which parts make you feel these emotions most strongly.

Activities

1. Were there any words that were difficult for you in the selection from *Kramer vs. Kramer*? Go back to these words and try to figure out their meanings. Discuss what you think each word means, and why you made that guess.

2. Are there any words new to you in the selection that you would like to remember? Discuss with your teacher or another student how you are going to remember each word. You could put them on file cards, or write them in your journal, or create a personal dictionary. Be sure to use each word in a sentence of your own.

3. How did you help yourself understand the selection? Did you ask yourself questions? What were they? Discuss these questions with other people who have read the same selection, or write about them in your journal.

4. Talking with other people about what you have read can increase your understanding of it. Discussion can help you organize your thoughts, get new ideas, and rethink your original ideas. Discuss your thoughts about the selection with someone else who has read it. Find out if your opinions are the same or different. See if your thoughts change as a result of this discussion.

5. If you like the selection, you might want to encourage someone else to read it. You could write a book review, or a letter to a friend you think might be interested in reading the book.

6. Did reading the selection give you any ideas for your own writing? You might want to write about:

   • your own relationship with a child or young friend.
   • a person you have known who is a single parent.
   • a time when you coped with an unexpected responsibility.

7. If you could talk to Avery Corman, what questions would you ask about his writing? You might want to write the questions in your journal.

8. What adjustments do children have to make when their parents divorce? What adjustments does an adult have to make when he or she is a single parent? How are the answers to these two questions the same? How are they different?

9. *Kramer vs. Kramer* shows that a father can be a good single parent. You might want to have a debate with other people. The title of the debate could be: "In a divorce, custody can be granted to the father, or the mother, or the parents jointly. Which is the best solution for the children?" One person could argue for the mother, another person for the father, and a third person for joint custody.

10. Is there something you kept thinking about after reading the selection? What? Write about why it is meaningful to you.

Resources

BIG BROTHERS/BIG SISTERS

117 South 17 Street
Philadelphia, PA 19103
(215) 567–7000 or look in your local phone directory

Big Brothers and Big Sisters have many groups
across the country. They match children with adult
volunteers who become special friends and role
models. This organization can be very helpful to a
single parent.

INTERNATIONAL YOUTH COUNCIL

8807 Colesbrille Road
Silver Spring, MD 20910
(301) 588–9354 or look in your local phone directory

International Youth Council has many groups
across the country. They provide support services for
teens whose parents are divorced or who have a
single parent.

NEW BEGINNINGS

612 Kennebec Avenue
Takoma Park, MD 20912
(301) 587–9233 or look in your local phone directory

New Beginnings has groups around the country.
They provide helpful information, as well as support
services for divorced men and women.

PARENTS ANONYMOUS

2230 Hawthorne Boulevard
Torrance, CA 90505
(800) 421–0353 or look in your local phone directory

Parents Anonymous has many groups across the
country. They also sponsor telephone hot lines. They
provide support for parents trying to cope with
their frustrations.

PARENTS WITHOUT PARTNERS

8807 Colesbrille Road
Silver Spring, MD 20910
(301) 588–9354 or look in your local phone directory

Parents Without Partners has many groups across
the country. They provide helpful information, as
well as support services for single parents.

Writers' Voices

☐ Rudolfo A. Anaya, *Selected from* BLESS ME, ULTIMA 0–929631–06–4 $2.95

☐ Maya Angelou, *Selected from* I KNOW WHY THE CAGED BIRD SINGS *and* THE HEART OF A WOMAN 0–929631–04–8 $2.95

☐ Carol Burnett, *Selected from* ONE MORE TIME 0–929631–03–X $2.95

☐ Avery Corman, *Selected from* KRAMER VS. KRAMER 0–929631–01–3 $2.95

☐ Bill Cosby, *Selected from* FATHERHOOD *and* TIME FLIES 0–929631–00–5 $2.95

☐ Louise Erdrich, *Selected from* LOVE MEDICINE 0–929631–02–1 $2.95

New Writers' Voices

☐ SPEAKING OUT ON HEALTH, *An Anthology* 0–929631–05–6 $2.95

To order any of these books, please send your check or money order (no cash, please) to Publishing Program, Literacy Volunteers of New York City Inc., Suite 520, 666 Broadway, New York, NY 10012. Please add $1.50 per order and 50¢ per book to cover postage and handling. New York and Connecticut residents, add appropriate sales tax. If you are a tax-exempt organization, include a copy of your exemption certificate with your order. For information on bulk discounts, please contact the Sales Manager at the above address.